ACTION
RHYMES

SELECTED BY SALLY EMERSON & PIE CORBETT

ILLUSTRATED BY MOIRA & COLIN MACLEAN

KINGFISHER

KINGFISHER
An imprint of Kingfisher Publications Plc
New Penderel House, 283-288 High Holborn
London WC1V 7HZ

First published by Kingfisher 1992
6 8 10 9 7
6TR/0103/AJT/-(FR)/150MA

The material in this edition was previously published by Kingfisher in
The Kingfisher Nursery Treasury (1988), *The Kingfisher Playtime Treasury* (1989)
and *The Kingfisher Nursery Songbook* (1991)

A CIP catalogue record for this book is available from the British Library.

ISBN 0 86272 889 4

Printed in India

CONTENTS

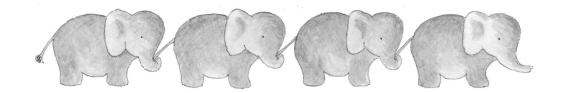

I'm a little teapot,
Short and stout,
Here's my handle,
Here's my spout.
When I see the teacups,
Hear me shout:
Tip me up and pour me out!

Do the actions as you sing.

  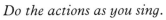 

I can tie my shoelaces,
I can brush my hair,
I can wash my face and hands
And dry myself with care.

I can clean my teeth, too,
And fasten up my frocks,
I can dress all by myself
And pull up both my socks.

The elephant goes
like this, like that,

He's terribly big,
And he's terribly fat.

He has no fingers,
He has no toes,

But goodness, gracious,
what a nose!

Mime the actions.

Handy Pandy,
Sugar Candy,
Which one will you choose,
Top or bottom?

*Hide something in one
hand. Then put one
closed fist over the other.
The game is to choose the
correct hand.*

Peter works with one hammer,
One hammer, one hammer;
Peter works with one hammer,
All day long.

Verses
Peter works with two hammers *etc.*
Peter works with three hammers *etc.*
Peter works with four hammers *etc.*
Peter works with five hammers *etc.*

*Hammer in time to the verse using one fist,
then two, then two fists and one foot, then
two fists and both feet. At FIVE, fists, feet
and head nod to the beat.*

Hurly burly trump a tray
  The goat was bought on market day.
Peter Piper hunt a buck.
  How many horns now stand up?

*One player covers her eyes while the other
holds up a number of fingers and chants the
rhyme. The game is to guess the number of
fingers held up.*

See-saw, Margery Daw,
Johnny shall have a new master;
He shall have but a penny a day,
Because he can't work any faster.

I can do the can-can just like this.
I can do the hoola hoop,
I can do the twist,
Queens go curtsey,
Kings go bow,
Boys go "Hi there!"
Girls go "Wow!"

This old man, he played one,
He played nick-nack on my drum.

Chorus
Nick-nack, paddy-whack,
Give a dog a bone
This old man came rolling home.

*Mime an appropriate action for each
verse. Repeat chorus after each verse.*

Verses

This old man, he played two,
He played nick-nack on my shoe.

This old man, he played three,
He played nick-nack on my knee.

This old man, he played four,
He played nick-nack on my door.

This old man, he played five,
He played nick-nack on my hide.

This old man, he played six,
He played nick-nack on some sticks.

This old man, he played seven,
He played nick-nack up to Heaven.

This old man, he played eight,
He played nick-nack at my gate.

This old man, he played nine,
He played nick-nack on my spine.

This old man, he played ten,
He played nick-nack once again.

Ring-a-ring o' roses,
A pocket full of posies,
A-tishoo! A-tishoo!
We all fall down.

*Choose either of the two second verses
to start again. Children will love
the race in the second version.*

The cows are in the meadow,
Eating buttercups,
A-tishoo! A-tishoo!
We all get up.

The cows are in the meadow,
Eating all the grass,
A-tishoo! A-tishoo!
Who's up last?
NOT ME!

Ride a cock-horse to Banbury Cross,
To see a fine lady upon a white horse;
Rings on her fingers,
And bells on her toes,
She shall have music
    wherever she goes.

Sally go round the sun,
Sally go round the moon,
Sally go round the chimney pots
On a Saturday afternoon.

*A good swinging rhyme. Also a favourite
for ring dancing.*

11

There was a man lived in the moon,
  lived in the moon, lived in the moon,
There was a man lived in the moon,
And his name was Aiken Drum.
And he played upon a ladle, a ladle, a ladle,
He played upon a ladle, and his name
  was Aiken Drum.

*Try singing this one while beating household
"instruments" such as spoons and saucepan lids.
Repeat the second verse changing the name of
the instrument each time. The traditional
verses describe Aiken Drum's clothes. Here are
some of them:*

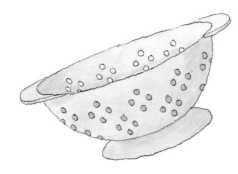

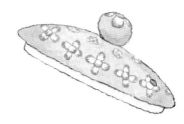

And his hat was made of good cream cheese,
  good cream cheese, good cream cheese,
And his hat was made of good cream cheese,
And his name was Aiken Drum.

And his coat was made of good roast beef,
  good roast beef, good roast beef,
And his coat was made of good roast beef,
And his name was Aiken Drum.

And his buttons were made of penny loaves,
  penny loaves, penny loaves,
And his buttons were made of penny loaves,
And his name was Aiken Drum.

We are off to Timbuctoo
Would you like to go there, too?
All the way and back again,
You must follow our leader then,
You must follow our leader,
You must follow our leader,
All the way and back again.
You must follow our leader.

*One person is chosen to be the leader
and everyone follows copying him.*

Polly Perkin, hold on to my jerkin
  Hold on to my gown,
That's the way we march to town.

Follow my Bangalory Man;
Follow my Bangalory Man;
I'll do all that I ever can
To follow my Bangalory Man.

We'll borrow a horse, and steal a gig,
And round the world we'll do a jig,
And I'll do all that I ever can
To follow my Bangalory Man.

Head and shoulders, knees and toes,
knees and toes,
Head and shoulders, knees and toes,
knees and toes.

*Touch each part of the
body as you sing.*

And eyes, and ears and mouth and nose,
Head and shoulders, knees and toes,
knees and toes.

If you're happy and you know it,
clap your hands.
If you're happy and you know it,
clap your hands.
If you're happy and you know it,
and you really want to show it,
If you're happy and you know it,
clap your hands.
If you're happy and you know it,
stamp your feet *etc.*
If you're happy and you know it,
nod your head *etc.*
If you're happy and you know it,
shout "Hooray!" *etc.*

Copy the actions.

1

2

Can you walk on tiptoe
As softly as a cat?

Can you stamp along the road
STAMP, STAMP, just like that?

3

4

Can you take some great big strides
Just like a giant can?

Or walk along so slowly,
Like a bent old man?

Stepping over stepping stones,
One, two, three,
Stepping over stepping stones,
Come with me.
The river's very fast,
And the river's very wide,
And we'll step across on stepping stones
And reach the other side.

Did you ever see a lassie,
A lassie, a lassie,
Did you ever see a lassie
Who acted like this?
This way and that way,
This way and that way,
Did you ever see a lassie
Who acted like this?

Mime the actions of the leader.
Change to laddie if a boy is the leader.

When I was a baby,
A baby, a baby,
When I was a baby
How happy I was.

Verses

When I was a lady,
A lady, a lady,
When I was a lady,
How happy I was.

Chorus

I was this way, and that way,
That way, and this way,
When I was a baby
Then this way went I.

When I was a sailor,
A sailor, a sailor,
When I was a sailor,
How happy I was.

Walk or skip while singing the first verse; stop for the
chorus and mime the verse. Repeat for each verse.

Miss Polly had a dolly
   who was sick, sick, sick,
So she phoned for the doctor
   to be quick, quick, quick.
The doctor came
   with her bag and her hat,
And she knocked on the door
   with a rat-a-tat-tat.

She looked at the dolly
   and she shook her head,
And she said, "Miss Polly,
   put her straight to bed."
She wrote on a paper
   for a pill, pill, pill,
"I'll be back in the morning
   with my bill, bill, bill."

Jack be nimble,
Jack be quick,
Jack JUMP over
   the candlestick.

Here am I,
   Little Jumping Joan;
When nobody's with me
   I'm all alone.

Handy Pandy, Jack-a-dandy,
Loves plum cake and sugar candy,
He bought some at the grocer's shop,
And out he came, hop, hop, hop!

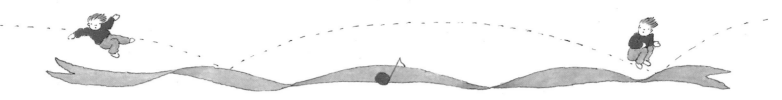

American jump! American jump!
One – Two – Three!
Under the water catching fishes,
Catching fishes for my tea.
    Dead . . .
    Or alive . . .
    Or around the world?

Holding a child under the arms or by the hands, jump her up three times. Catch her around your waist at THREE, then lower her backwards to catch a fish, and offer a choice of "Dead or alive or around the world".
For DEAD, lower her to the ground.
For ALIVE, swing her up high.
For AROUND THE WORLD, swing her over your back and down again.

Round and round the rugged rock
The ragged rascal ran.
How many R's are there in that?
Now tell me if you can.

I have a dog and his name is Rags,
He eats so much that his tummy sags,
His ears flip-flop,
And his tail wig-wags,
And when he walks he goes zig-zag.

Chorus

He goes flip-flop, wig-wag, zig-zag,
He goes flip-flop, wig-wag, zig-zag,
He goes flip-flop, wig-wag, zig-zag,
I love Rags and he loves me.
I love Rags and he loves me.

My dog Rags he loves to play
He rolls around in the mud all day.
I whistle but he won't obey.
He always runs the other way.

*Follow the actions using hands and fingers
to imitate the words. Hands at either side of
head drop forwards for FLIP-FLOP; hips wiggle
for WIG-WAG; arms cross for ZIG-ZAG; hands
rotate for ROLLS AROUND; fingers wiggle for
RUNS THE OTHER WAY and so on.*

Little Rabbit Foo Foo
Hopping through the green grass,
Scooping up the field mice,
Knocking them on the head.

*Everyone sits in a circle and two players
are chosen to be RABBIT FOO FOO and the
GOOD FAIRY. Rabbit Foo Foo hops inside the
circle pretending to scoop up mice. Then the
Good Fairy arrives and gives her a number
of chances.*

Down came the Good Fairy
And she said:
Little Rabbit Foo Foo,
I don't want to see you,
Scooping up the field mice,
Knocking them on the head,
So I'll give you *three* more chances.

Little Rabbit Foo Foo
I really warned you;
Now I'm going to turn you
Into a *red-eyed monster*.

*The first two verses are repeated with the
Good Fairy appearing each time to count the
number of chances left. When these are used
up the Good Fairy decides what to turn
Rabbit Foo Foo into . . . a monster, a frog . . . ?*

Choose two players to be ROGER and the OLD LADY.

Old Roger is dead and he lies in his grave,
Lies in his grave, lies in his grave.
Old Roger is dead and he lies in his grave,
Heigh ho, lies in his grave.

They planted an apple tree over his head,
Over his head, over his head.
They planted an apple tree over his head,
Heigh ho, over his head.

The apples grew ripe and they all tumbled down,
All tumbled down, all tumbled down.
The apples grew ripe and they all tumbled down;
Heigh ho, they all tumbled down.

There came an old woman a-picking them up,
A-picking them up, a-picking them up.
There came an old woman a-picking them up,
Heigh ho, a-picking them up.

Old Roger got up and he gave her a knock,
Gave her a knock, gave her a knock.
Old Roger got up and he gave her a knock,
Heigh ho, gave her a knock.

This made the old woman go hipperty-hop,
Hipperty-hop, hipperty-hop,
This made the old woman go hipperty-hop,
Heigh ho, hipperty-hop.

Here is the church,	Here is the parson
And here is the steeple,	Going upstairs,
Open the doors,	And here is the parson
And here are the people.	Saying his prayers.

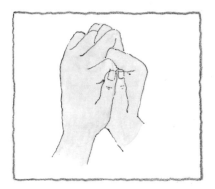

Interlock fingers.

Raise index fingers.

Open thumbs and wriggle fingers.

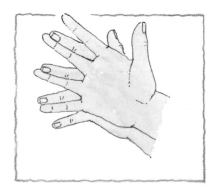

Undo hands. Cross wrists and interlace fingers back to back.

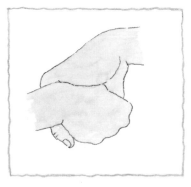

Rotate wrists until palms face each other, fingers curled inside.

Wriggle thumb.

Incey wincey spider
Climbing up the spout,
Down came the rain
And washed the spider out.

Out came the sunshine,
Dried up all the rain,
Incey Wincey spider
Climbing up again.

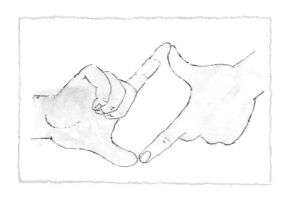

*Climb up by touching opposite
thumb and index fingers.*

Snail, snail, put out your horns,
And I'll give you bread and barley corns.

*Make a fist, tucking your thumb inside. Lift
little finger and index finger to make horns.*

Oh, the grand old Duke of York,
He had ten thousand men.
He marched them up
to the top of the hill
And he marched them down again.

And when they were up they were up,
And when they were down they were down,
And when they were only half-way up
They were neither up nor down.

March in time, jumping UP and crouching
DOWN, and acting out the additional verses below.
Repeat the second verse after each new verse.

Oh, the grand old Duke of York,
He had ten thousand men.
They beat their drums
to the top of the hill
And they beat them down again.

They played their pipes to the top of the hill *etc.*
They banged their guns to the top of the hill *etc.*

Frère Jacques, Frère Jacques,
Dormez-vous? Dormez-vous?
Sonnez les matines,
Sonnez les matines,
Din, din, don! Din, din, don!

I hear thunder, I hear thunder.
Hark, don't you? Hark don't you?
Pitter patter raindrops,
Pitter patter raindrops,
I'm wet through, so are you.

*Drum with hands or feet; stop and
listen; flutter fingers; hug, as if cold.*

*A very popular round song: after the
first singer has sung the first line, the
second singer starts while the first
continues on to the next line. The
English alternative below can be sung
with actions.*

I see blue skies, I see blue skies,
Way up high, way up high.
Hurry up now sunshine,
Hurry up now sunshine.
I'll soon dry, I'll soon dry.

*Look up, and point to the sky; make
the circle of the sun; shake hands dry.*

The wheels on the bus go round and round,
Round and round, round and round.
The wheels on the bus go round and round,
All day long.

Rotate arms like wheels.

The wipers on the bus go swish, swish, swish,
Swish, swish, swish, swish, swish, swish.
The wipers on the bus go swish, swish, swish,
All day long.

Wave hands from side to side.

Other verses
The people on the bus go:
  Yakkity-yak! *etc.*

Open and shut fingers and thumb.

The driver on the bus goes:
  Toot, toot, toot *etc.*

Press imaginary horn with thumb.

The children on the bus make
too much NOISE *etc.*

Hands over ears and shout NOISE.

The babies on the bus fall
fast asleep *etc.*

Head on hands as if asleep, and whisper lines.

INDEX OF FIRST LINES